I AM NOT A FROG

NOT A FROG

MAGGIE PEARSON
ILLUSTRATED BY NATALIA MOORE

BLOOMSBURY EDUCATION
Bloomsbury Publishing Plc
50 Bedford Square, London, WC1B 3DP, UK

BLOOMSBURY, BLOOMSBURY EDUCATION and the Diana logo are
trademarks of Bloomsbury Publishing Plc

First published in Great Britain 2019 by Bloomsbury Publishing Plc
Text copyright © Maggie Pearson, 2019
Illustrations copyright © Natalia Moore, 2019

Maggie Pearson and Natalia Moore have asserted their rights under the Copyright, Designs and
Patents Act, 1988, to be identified as Authors and Illustrator of this work

A catalogue record for this book is available from the British Library

ISBN: PB: 978-1-4729-5976-8; ePDF: 978-1-4729-5977-5; ePub: 978-1-4729-5975-1
enhanced ePub: 978-1-4729-6951-4

2 4 6 8 10 9 7 5 3 1

Printed and bound in China by Leo Paper Products, Heshan, Guangdong

All papers used by Bloomsbury Publishing Plc are natural, recyclable products from wood
grown in well managed forests. The manufacturing processes conform to the environmental
regulations of the country of origin

To find out more about our authors and books visit www.bloomsbury.com
and sign up for our newsletters

Chapter One

"Why can't I go outside the palace?" demanded Princess Imelda for the umpteenth time.

For the umpteenth time the queen answered, "Because outside is where the common people live."

"You are a princess," said the king.
"One day you will be Queen of Livia."
Livia is a very small country. The
king and queen made up for having
such a small country by being very,
very grand.
"Hmph!" said Imelda.

Carefully she planned her escape.
This is how she did it.
Six little girls came to her
birthday party.
(Pay attention now.
This is important.)
Anastasia came in
a blue dress.
Agatha's dress was red.
Gwendolyn's was green.

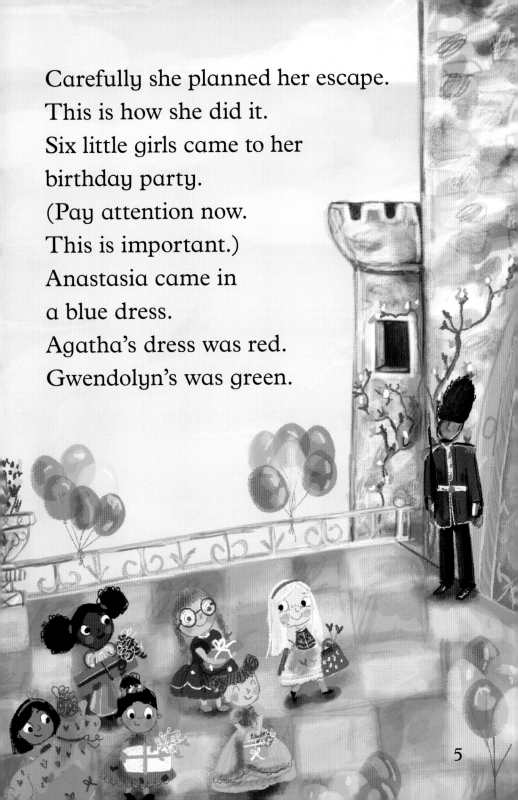

Mitzi was in lilac, Fritzi wore turquoise and Poppy came dressed in orange.
Imelda's dress was yellow.
Imelda said to Anastasia, "What a pretty dress! Can I try it on?"
"Can I try yours?" said Anastasia.

"Of course," said Imelda. "And the crown as well."

Soon they were all joining in.

Seven little girls sat down to tea pretending to be each other and took turns wearing the crown.

When they went home they were still wearing each other's dresses.

(Are you still paying attention?)
Anastasia left the party dressed in green. Mitzi wore orange and Fritzi was in yellow.

Imelda wore Anastasia's blue. After her came Gwendolyn, Poppy and Agatha, dressed in red and lilac and turquoise.

"So who was the one in blue?" said one of the guards to the other.

"That was Anastasia."

"I thought she was the one in green."

"I call it blue. You call it green."

"And I only counted six going in."

"Six or seven. Let's not make a fuss."

9

Chapter Two

Upstairs the crown lay on the table. A small, green frog hopped out of the bathroom. It hopped onto a chair, onto the table and sat inside the crown, looking out.
The queen came in, saw the frog and screamed.

"The princess! Princess Imelda has been turned into a frog!"
"Perhaps it was something she ate," said the king.

Imelda hadn't eaten anything. She'd been too excited. She wandered through the town, looking at the shops, the traffic and the people. So many people!

At last she did get hungry. She looked through a window and saw a lot of people eating. So in she went, sat down and ate until she was full.

The waiter brought the bill.
"What's this?" said Imelda.
"You haven't paid," he said.
"I haven't what?" said Imelda.
"Paid," said the waiter.
"With money."
"With what?" said Imelda.
"This stuff!" said the
waiter, showing her the
coins in his pocket.

Imelda was a princess.
She'd never seen money
before – she had never needed it.

The waiter sent for the cook.
"If you can't pay the bill," said the
cook, "you can wash up instead."
"Thank you," said Imelda.
She'd never washed up before.
Washing up was fun.

By the time she'd finished, everyone else had gone. She was so tired, she curled up by the fire and fell asleep.

Chapter Three

Next morning the news was in all the papers.

The queue of people offering to change her back stretched right round the palace.

Some of them gave the frog medicine
to drink. Some dunked it *in* the
medicine.

One or two tried kissing it better.
One danced round it banging a
drum until the queen said it gave
her a headache.

Last of all came The Great Ravioli.
"Looks like some kind of stage
magician," muttered the king.
"Perhaps a touch of magic is what we
need," whispered the queen.
"Your highness!" said Ravioli,
smiling, leaning close
to the frog.

The frog hopped backwards.
"Erk?" it said.
The Great Ravioli nodded wisely.
"Can you change her back?"
said the king.
"Only if she wants to change
back," said Ravioli.

"You mean she's doing it
on purpose?" exclaimed
the queen. "Imelda, stop
this silly game at once."

19

"Erk?" said the frog.

"Sh!" said The Great Ravioli. "Dear lady, that's not the modern way. If she wants to be a frog, you must let her. Let's start with a bath in the pond. And a meal of bluebottles. She'll soon get tired of cold baths and eating flies."

Chapter Four

Imelda soon got tired of washing up.
And peeling potatoes and chopping
onions and scrubbing floors.
A few days later she went and knocked
on the door of the palace.
"It's me," said Imelda. "I've come home."

The guards sent
for Ravioli.
"Who are you?"
said Imelda.
"I am The Great Ravioli."
"And I am Princess
Imelda. Now can I come
in, please?"

Ravioli said, "You are not a princess. A princess always keeps herself neat and clean. Besides, Princess Imelda is upstairs."

"That's just a frog," said Imelda. "I was keeping it in the bathroom."

"That frog is your princess!" cried Ravioli. "Go away, little common person before I have you arrested!"

The door slammed.

"Hmph!" said Imelda. "Either that frog goes or I do... Maybe I will go. I can travel the world and have adventures. One day I'll come back and claim my throne."

Off she went, down the road out of town, towards the border. She didn't get very far before she began to have an adventure. A boy dropped out of a tree in front of her.

Another boy sprang over the hedge.

A third tumbled out of a dustbin.
"This is an ambush!" they yelled. "Put
your hands up and give us your money!"

"How can I give you my money if I've
got my hands up?"
"All right," said the first boy. "You can
put your hands down."
"Now give us your money," said the
second boy.

"Why?" said Imelda.

"Because we're outlaws. We steal from the rich to give to the poor," said the first boy.

"I'm poor," said Imelda. "I've got no money at all. Can you give me some?"

"Sorry," said the first boy. "We've got no money either."

"This is our first day," said the second boy. "And our first ambush."

"We're outlaws," said the littlest one.
"Why?" said Imelda.
"Because we don't want a frog for a princess. One day that frog will be queen! How daft is that?"
"I think I can help you there," said Imelda. "I am the true Princess Imelda! Ta-da!"

The outlaws looked at her in her
grubby dress.
"You're not," they said.
"I am," she said. "And you can help me
reclaim my throne."
The outlaws looked at one another.
"At least she's not a frog," said one.

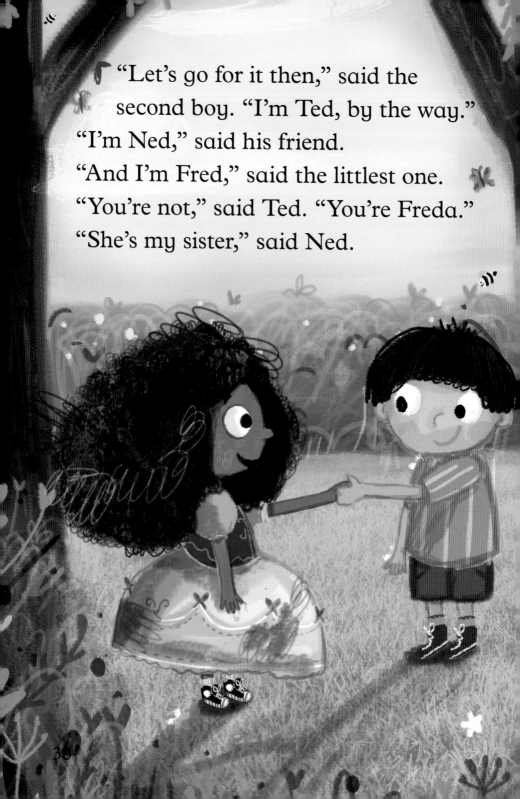

"Let's go for it then," said the
second boy. "I'm Ted, by the way."
"I'm Ned," said his friend.
"And I'm Fred," said the littlest one.
"You're not," said Ted. "You're Freda."
"She's my sister," said Ned.

"I'm Fred," the littlest one
said firmly.
"Pleased to meet you, Fred," said
Imelda. "You too Ned. And Ted."
"We've got a camp," said Fred.
"Come and see."

Chapter Five

Back at the palace, the queen spent most of her time bathing the frog in the pond.

The king hopped and skipped round the garden, catching flies for it to eat.

The frog stayed what it
was always meant to be. A frog.
The Great Ravioli smiled a sinister
smile. His plan was working nicely.
"Have you got any more bright ideas?"
said the king.

"It seems," said Ravioli, "that the princess is happy being a frog. So let's celebrate!"

"Let's what?" said the queen.

"Let's show her to her people!"

"As a frog?" said the king.

"As a frog," said Ravioli. "Add in the crown jewels, and fireworks afterwards, and free ice cream… people will soon get used to the idea."

"There's going to be a procession!"
said Ted. "With a band and kids
dancing and soldiers marching –"
"And fireworks afterwards and free ice
cream!" said Fred.
"And the princess in a carriage driven
by Ravioli," said Ned. "With the crown
and all the crown jewels."

FROG
PRINCESS

"What's he up to?" said Ned.
"I know!" cried Fred. "I saw him
through a window. He was looking
at a map. 'Two days more,' he
said to himself, 'and I'll be a very
rich man.' Two days more, that's
the day of the procession."

"He's going to steal the crown jewels!" said Ted.

"Not if we can stop him!" said Ned.

This, thought Imelda, *is my chance to get rid of that frog!*

Chapter Six

The big day came.
Crowds lined the streets.
They cheered and waved little flags.
The town band played, the children
danced along and the army marched
behind, all twelve of them. (Livia is a
very small country, remember.)

Last came the royal carriage, driven by
The Great Ravioli.
In it sat the frog with the crown over it,
inside a little golden cage. All around
lay the rest of the crown jewels.
"Ooo!" cried the crowd, and "Aaah!"
as the crown jewels went past.

"Aha!" Ravioli chuckled as he reached the crossroads and the road leading back into town.
The band turned left.
The children followed.
The army began marching after them.

Ravioli drove on, down
the road to the border.
The army stopped.
"Stop, thief!" yelled
the captain.
The carriage went faster.
After it ran the army…
the schoolchildren…
the band… and the
townspeople.

"Stop thief! He's stealing the princess –
and the crown jewels."
Back at the palace the king and queen
stood on the balcony, ready to wave
as the procession marched by. They
wondered where everybody had gone.

Ravioli knew where he was going.
Over the hills to somewhere sunny,
where he'd be a very rich man.
Until he turned a corner and saw a
landslide! A barricade! An ambush!
"Stand and deliver!" cried the outlaws.

"We're arresting you, you crook,"
said Fred.
"For stealing the crown jewels,"
said Ted.
"And kidnapping the princess!"
added Ned.

"That's not the princess," sneered Ravioli. "That's just a fr– oh!"

"A what?" said Imelda. There she sat in the carriage with the crown on her head and the royal robes wrapped round her. The procession marched back into town, with The Great Ravioli under arrest.

The people cheered and waved their
flags harder than ever.

"Imelda, darling!" cried the queen.
"So nice to see you looking your old
self again," said the king. "That fellow
Ravioli was a crook, but he did know
something about children."

Meanwhile, in a muddy ditch, a small green frog was having a quiet lie down, wondering if it had once been a princess or whether it had only dreamed it all.